Based on the episode written by Kurt Redeker
Adapted by Sheila Sweeny Higginson
Illustrated by Alan Batson

This edition published by Parragon Books Ltd in 2015

Parragon Books Ltd
Chartist House
15–17 Trim Street
Bath BA1 1HA, UK
www.parragon.com

ISBN 978-1-4748-1384-6

Printed in China

Bubble Trouble

Bath • New York • Cologne • Melbourne • Delhi
Hong Kong • Shenzhen • Singapore • Amsterdam

Doc likes to play with her best friend Emmie and her little sister Alma. One of their favourite toys is a Bubble Monkey bubble blower.

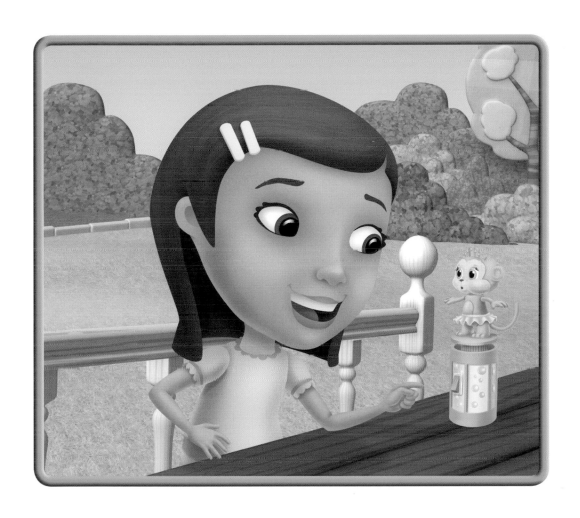

Emmie puts Bubble Monkey on the picnic table and flips her switch. Three...two...one...

Bubbles, bubbles everywhere!
Alma pops three bubbles, and Emmie pops six.
Doc pops two bubbles at once!

Emmie's dog Rudi wants to pop bubbles, too.
But Bubble Monkey isn't working anymore.
She's all out of bubbles.

Alma fills up Bubble Monkey while Doc and Emmie chase after Rudi. When she's done, she asks, "Is everyone ready?" They are!

Three...two...one...
But no bubbles!

"Where are the bubbles?" asks Alma.
"I'll take a look and see if I can figure
out what's wrong," says Doc.

Doc takes Bubble Monkey to her clinic and brings her to life with her magic stethoscope.

"Hey, look!" Stuffy says. "Doc brought Bubble Monkey over to play."

"Sorry, Stuffy, but Bubble Monkey is here for a checkup," says Doc.

First, Doc runs some tests and takes a feather from her bag. She asks Bubble Monkey to blow it.

Bubble Monkey blows, but the feather barely moves.

"Let the dragon try it!" says Stuffy.
Stuffy blows the feather right out of Doc's hand!
It lands on Chilly's face.
"Achoo!" Chilly sneezes.

Next, Doc listens to Bubble Monkey's chest.
"Sounds like goop is blocking your bubble pumper," she says.
"Are you having any other symptoms?"
"What are symptoms?" asks Bubble Monkey.

Doc explains that symptoms are things that hurt.
"It's your body's way of telling you that something
is wrong."
"Well, I have a tummy ache," Bubble Monkey says.

"Can I give your tummy a little squeeze?" Doc asks.
She presses Bubble Monkey's stomach.
Something shoots out and hits Stuffy in the chest.
"Ick!" says Stuffy.

Now Stuffy and Chilly are stuck together!
"Weird," says Doc as she pulls them apart.
"This is paste."

Doc heads back to Emmie's garden to investigate. "Alma, what did you put in Bubble Monkey?" she asks.

Alma holds up the pink jar. "I used this," she says.
"Alma, the pink one is paste!" Emmie says.
"The green one is the bubble soap!"

Doc rushes back to the clinic.
"I have a diagnosis!" she tells Bubble Monkey.
"You have a bad case of Gunk-inside-atude."

"Toys need to get filled right, just like people need to eat right," says Doc.

Then Doc cleans out Bubble Monkey's tubes and fills her up with bubble soap.

"Thanks, Doc. I feel better!"
"You're super fantastic!" Bubble Monkey cheers.

"I love my job!" says Doc.
"Now let's get you back to Emmie and Alma."

"I'm back!" Doc says.
"And this time, I brought Bubble Monkey!"

"Did you fix her?" Alma asks.
"There's only one way to find out," says Doc.
Three...two...one...

Bubbles!